THE WEAK

THE WEAKNESS

Bernard O'Donoghue

Chatto & Windus
LONDON

Published in 1991 by
Chatto & Windus Ltd
20 Vauxhall Bridge Road
London SW1V 2SA

A CIP catalogue record for this book is available
from the British Library

ISBN 0 7011 3859 9

Some of the poems in this volume appeared in the shorter
collections *Razorblades and Pencils* (Sycamore Press, 1984),
Poaching Rights (Gallery Press, Dublin, 1987) and *The
Absent Signifier* (Mandeville Press, 1990). Acknowledgments
are also due to the editors of the following magazines and
anthologies where other poems appeared for the first time:
The Irish Reporter; *Irish University Review*; *The Kerryman*;
'New Irish Writing' (*The Sunday Tribune*); *The Oxford
Magazine*; *Oxford Poetry*; *Poetry Durham*; *Poetry Ireland
Review*; *The Poetry Book Society Anthology 1988–1989*; *The
Poetry Book Society Anthology 1991*; *Sanity*; *The Times
Literary Supplement*.

Photoset by
Cambridge Composing (UK) Ltd
Cambridge

Printed and bound in Great Britain by
Mackays of Chatham PLC, Chatham, Kent

Contents

III Maladies

I IMMATURITIES

A NUN TAKES THE VEIL

That morning early I ran through briars
To catch the calves that were bound for market.
I stopped the once, to watch the sun
Rising over Doolin across the water.

The calves were tethered outside the house
While I had my breakfast: the last one at home
For forty years. I had what I wanted (they said
I could), so we'd loaf bread and Marie biscuits.

We strung the calves behind the boat,
Me keeping clear to protect my style:
Confirmation suit and my patent sandals.
But I trailed my fingers in the cool green water,

Watching the puffins driving homeward
To their nests on Aran. On the Galway mainland
I tiptoed clear of the cow-dunged slipway
And watched my brothers heaving the calves

As they lost their footing. We went in a trap,
Myself and my mother, and I said goodbye
To my father then. The last I saw of him
Was a hat and jacket and a salley stick,

Driving cattle to Ballyvaughan.
He died (they told me) in the county home,
Asking to see me. But that was later:
As we trotted on through the morning mist,

I saw a car for the first time ever,
Hardly seeing it before it vanished.
I couldn't believe it, and I stood up looking
To where I could hear its noise departing

But it was only a glimpse. That night in the convent
The sisters spoilt me, but I couldn't forget
The morning's vision, and I fell asleep
With the engine humming through the open window.

THE POULTRY INSTRUCTRESSES

They felt the cold much more than other people
And huddled by the fire in smart coats
And 'New Look' frocks, brooding bitterly
On hens. Their very names declared them meant
For something better: Hutchinson or Dunn
Or Hervey. If they'd been boys, or born
In another age, they'd have been put on
For the church or a dignified profession.

As it was, after a cup of tea, they stood
In disdain with needle poised in the flurry
Of Leghorn and Rhode Island Red which had to be
Bloodtested and ringed, while the locals plunged
And clutched round the henhouse like bad goalkeepers.
All minds on escape: for how could anyone
Hope to teach a hen or hen-farmer anything?

Once, attacked by pre-school shyness, I ran
To seize my mother's skirt and knee, and felt
The soft, perfumed friction of fine nylons.
I'd embraced Miss Dunn in full view of everyone.

NOMINATIONS ARE INVITED

There are people around so blind they couldn't tell
Przewalski's horse from Willie Casey's jennet.
Though Dominic's next to us had guinea-hens
Calling 'Two clock! Two clock!' and a mauve turkey
Whose nose ran red skin continuously,
Our local book of field birds was transcribed
In a broad script: crow, duck or sparrow.
Poor inheritors of the gift of Adam.

On the way into the zoo, you'd never seek
The route shown in the map, but use directions
From somebody whose cousin went there once
Years ago. Emerging through the entrance,
You couldn't put a name to any species.

Yet still there lingered on behind your eye
Something the past or present left around
The place. Big cats in snow: a curiosity
There for you. Or some bird's dart of colour
Recalling fairy thimbles or dead man's fingers,
Purple and orange and hung with cuckoo spit.

O'REGAN THE AMATEUR ANATOMIST

The gander clapped out its flat despair
While O'Regan sawed at its legs with his penknife.
He looked at me with a friendly smile as blood
Dripped in huge, dark drips. I didn't protest
Or flail out at him, but smiled in return,
Knowing what grown-ups do, whatever breeds
About their hearts, is always for the best.
Worms are cold-blooded; babies learn in the night
By being left to cry. Another time (a man
So generous, they said, he'd give you the sweet
From his mouth) he halved a robin with that knife.
Finally, racing his brother back from a funeral
Down a darkening road he drove his car
Under a lightless lorry, cutting his head off.
I wonder what he thought he was up to then?

FINN THE BONESETTER

Proverbial wisdom kept us off the streets
And that's a fact. The art of talk is dead.
When we had shaken all our heads enough
At people's knowing in the days of old
(When a cow died they thanked Almighty God
It wasn't one of them), we'd contemplate
Our local marvel-workers. On the flat
Of his back for three years and more, surgeons
Could do nothing: Finn had him walking
The four miles to Mass inside an hour.

Incurably rheumatical myself,
I made him out at home above Rockchapel
Where the swallows purred approving in the eaves.
Bent at a crystal mirror, he was bathing
A red eye. 'I'm praying I won't go blind
From it. Do you know anything about eyes?'
Beyond having heard it said that his descried
The future, I didn't. He rolled his sleeves
Back to his shoulder like an accredited
Inseminator and got down to it.
I'm such relieved and think there's something in it.

BIG BOYS

'There are no big boys now like there used to be',
Denny-John said to me in 1954
When he was eleven and I was eight.
He reeled off their names: boys who wore long trousers
And reared menacingly above you. Boys who would
    break
Into the school over the weekend and steal the stick
With which the master smashed the palms of children
Who couldn't spell 'separate' or 'hesitency'.
Boys whose voices were breaking, one of whom
Was grey at fourteen. Boys who would scorn to wear
Shoes and socks, come rain, frost or hail. Nowadays
Six-year-olds wore long trousers, and their mothers
Kissed them as they left home, pushing a hankie
Or a hound-stamped sixpence into their palms.
We that were so young would never see so much
Nor live so long as to be apprenticed at twelve,
Or on the emigrant high seas at seventeen.

PISHEOGUE MASTER

Tonight by the hearth the wind gave up the ghost,
Letting the ash drift and signalling
Unventilated blight-mist in the morning,

Good for my purpose. So I'll take the eggs,
Abandoned by the hen who was laying out
Under the blackthorn. There they sat for months,

Snuffed nightly by the hungry fox and left,
Thirteen cold *gliogars* with the reassuring scent
Of H_2S. I must not see myself

As I fold the rancid butter in my coat
And slide from its sock the orange-bottle, full
Of slime-twining water from the sick calf's bed.

Everything must be said and nothing seen.
Sprinkle the water on the boundary fence;
Smear the butter on the pumptree. Listen (shush!)

To their child wheezing as her chest constricts:
My ill-luck, maybe, already on the wing.
Tuck up the loveless eggs in my rotting hay

To make a swaddling-bundle with soft words
And bear it past the hedges to bequeath
Its damp heat deep in the neighbouring barns.

Then tomorrow I'll look all men in the eye,
Despising their priestly superstitions and
Their cowering aspersions on my faith.

The air begins to brighten. In the tree
The thrush is wakened up by his own singing.
Stealing home unmissed, I notice the stone

Supporting my slumped gate has rolled away.
I see these things as omens and take hope;
If my sick wife should die, I'd die of grief.

EX CORDE

On All Souls Day for every call you made
To the village chapel (each re-entry
Counting technically as another visit),
Some blessed soul sailed to eternal glory
Amid general rejoicing; for God
In his infinite whimsy can't resist
The sight of innocent children shoving
And sniggering in and out the door.
You could save twenty in an afternoon.

Despite misgivings, you would never say
That the procedure seemed a bit easy
Compared to standing in sackcloth and ashes
For three hundred days, or even to thinning
Turnips with sackcloth wound around your knees.
You're not going to change a system which pays off
So liberally, standing you in good stead
With parents, teachers, deity and the grave.
It's not for us to question the Almighty's
Taxing system. His ways are not our ways,
Even if they're suspiciously reminiscent.

GRANARY

On the newwood floor of the grainloft
The oats shine lunar-blue, a drift
Like dry sand blown back from the sea.

Close a hand over the grain
And it teems like solid wine
Through the fingers. Yeats in London

Used to hold a shard of Sligo
In his palm, shoring such fragments
Against his ruin: so the last day there

I stored a fistful in my pocket.
Today by chance I found it:
It pierced like splinters of glass

Beneath my nails, leaving only
Grizzled chaff to complicate
The dull, tweed weave of my coat.

IMMATURITIES

My Manchester mother was a City fan,
So I'm one too. Once, as Wembley sang
'Abide With Me' (only, my father said,
Upsetting people), she shockingly
Ran crying from our Irish kitchen.

But when, that February, ice on the wing
Caused the United plane to crash,
Club differences were dropped. Cuttings came
From the *Evening News* about the Sheffield match,
Reporting 'a ghost in every red shirt'.

The milk-windows of ice cracked beneath
Our heels as we, local celebrities,
Walked to the shop. – Was our mother upset? –
Not really. (You couldn't admit as much.)
There was another, similar vapouring

When Regan set the black dog swinging
From the friesian's tail. Her hind legs splayed
In the dust, making her ample milk-bag
Look ridiculous. My mother clutched her ears
And stamped and screamed. Such a display in public!

And then, when my father died, we wondered
Driving home if those half-hushed night arguments
Meant she'd take it with indifference.
But when we opened the door, we thought the noise
That greeted us was a mad cow roaring.

MADE IN ENGLAND

The pulper still outside the window
Blocking the light, twenty years since
Its handle turned and the last droppings
Fell from it. 'English stuff costs more' –
Tracing the cast-iron, proud legend
Bamford – 'but it lasts the longest.
Like the BSA frame, guaranteed
For ever.' But few in this inch
Of Atlantean West Cork
Could stay the pace with it.

LESSER DEATHS

to Josie

So it's farewell to Ballybunion,
Will I ever see thee more?

A memory lingers without evident point
Of my father one ordinary morning
Conveying me the road to school
As far as the turn, to check the cows were
Safely grazing in the right field,
Shepherded by the steady pulse
Of the electric fence, and then
Turning back as I walked on. Once
I turned to see his back steadily
Walking from me and was pierced
By a knife which twisted years after
When his heart stopped beating. Now,
Josie, sand-absorbed, hands me a spade,
Laughing, chattering: then slams thumb
In mouth with a silent stare when I say
I must leave her and go to work.

TOM'S SOLDIERS

A humming Gulliver, spreadeagled in
The carpet's geometry, surrounded
By plastic personnel with arms levelled:
Two hundred plus, ten per 90p platoon,
And reinforced weekly. His thoughtful heels
Kick out a strategy, accompanied
By quiet, palatal-fricative explosions.

But where will it end? The obsessional,
If I remember rightly, continues
With football; stamp-collecting; God; the dog;
Music; sex; and our present crotchety,
Opinionated lives. Farther than that
I can't predict for him, still waiting myself
For reason's horses to declare the outcome.

ELLEN'S CLOCK

She never fails to set her alarm,
Herself a clock that, through the night
If you wake up, reassures you
By its ticking that the house is still alive.

But sometimes, in the early hours,
You lie, listening to its regularity
In terror, lest each tick might be its last.

THE DANDY DOLLS

from George Fitzmaurice

At one time I could have told you plainly
The reason for making them, but now it's gone
From me. Something to do with luck.

But the ritual's still the same: first of all
I eat the stolen geese, because it was they
Who warned the Capitol. Then I lie down

For three days in stupor. When I wake up
I work without sleep or eating till she's done
Completely: two careful thread crosses

For eyes; floppy neck and stitched shoulders
Which must be fingered gently. This new doll's
The best one yet – the latest always is.

Maybe she'll survive. Maybe the wind's too strong
For the hag's destructive son to ride here
From the shore of Doon for her, to tear out

Her windpipe to blow mockery through
For the grey brotherhood by the sea.
In hopes that she'll survive, I'll name her:

Mommet's been tried before, and *Abigail*.
A name that betrayed her less would let her hide
Among the rest of us and live such life

As could be hers. What name might that be?
But as the clock strikes out this hour of truth,
I know she'll no more last than did the rest.

LEPIDUS TIMIDUS HIBERNICUS

Familiar of ditches, coming and going
Over the headland in the boggy acre
Where his form is. A bird of ill omen,
The old woman said, blessing herself.
There he goes (if you have the misfortune
To see him), pulsing away, tan brown
As the wary wren on the polish tin.

'I bless myself because, if he is shot
In the leg, they say I, here in my kitchen
Coven, will find my shoe filling with blood
While I comb out increasingly white tresses'.

Which is maybe why it's with our blessing that
Greyhounds slaver in their slipstream to savage
These initiates that spring vibrant from the last
Golden sheaf: such awesome cabbage-stags
Or furze-cats as preside in their hundreds
At Aldergrove, while the jet's whine rises
To hysteria, before taking soldiers
Or civilians towards death or joy or injury.

THE APPARITION

More surprising than a moving statue
Of the Blessed Virgin, that yellow plane
Stationary in an Irish farmer's field
In the 'fifties: a four-day shrine until
Its tilted take-off, a wing-heavy heron.

That wasn't the end of it: disputation
Ran for months about its origins: what age
It came from, or what place; in what hangar
It wintered, north or south; whether our climate
Was too hot or cold for it: too dry or wet.

Last night I dreamt I saw it once again,
Thirty years later, on an empty patch
Beside the jumbo runway at Heathrow
From the window of a transatlantic jet
Through the pre-departure gauze of heat.

I tried to call 'what message have you brought
From Bill Casey's field?' But the Boeing's whine
Defeated me as it carefully conducted
Its slow, elephantine pirouette.
Accepting that I'd never hear the truth,

I settled back to study our flight-path;
But as we drifted past it, gathering speed,
I saw clearly the notice I'd forgotten
Chalked on cardboard in the pilot's seat:
'Out of fuel. Back when we've got some more'.

II SECOND THOUGHTS

THE STATE OF THE NATION

*'The condition upon which God hath given liberty to
  man is eternal vigilance'* (John Philpot Curran, 1790)

Before I fell asleep, I had been reading
How in the Concentration Camps, alongside
The Jewish personal effects, were stored
For future reference gipsies' earrings,
Scarves and the crystal globes in which they saw
The future; and how the Guardia Civil
Swept through Fuente Vaqueros, smashing guitars.

The book was open still when I woke up
At dawn and, not reassured by the May chorus
From the cypresses, ran to the encampment
At the crossroads where slow smoke curled by the sign
'Temporary Dwellings Prohibited'.
Still there; spread in dew along the hedges
Were gossamer and shawls and tea-towels.

A chained dog watched me peering under
The first canvas flap. Empty. The rest the same.
Not a soul in any tent. I straightened up
And listened through the sounds of morning
For voices raised in family rows, or their ponies
Tocking back from venial raids, bringing home
Hay, a clutch of eggs, unminded pullets.

THE USUAL SUSPECTS

The patent stuff I spray on the flowers
Makes insects lose all reason. Instead
Of escaping, they leap at the nozzle
Till all their green cadavers lie soused
In their rosewood bedrooms. The roses
Are no better: they jag and tear at the hand
That risks the faecal dampness to pull out
The choking clover, bringing their roots air.

Last night's electric storm came just when their buds
Were opening and the peony's crimson egg
Was splitting to give birth. In the morning
The peony lies prone, the rosebuds shrivelled
And the dead greenfly are all washed away.
The clover prospers silently. It defeats
The roses to know who to blame, since

When you hear something, that's nothing.
When you hear nothing, that's the Indian.

POMPEIANA

Scratching away for shards of singed, green tile,
They'll be trying to assemble Sunday mornings
From our pre-atomic age. Infinitely
Careful, they'll fit them all together
To display medals and competition shields,
Serenaded by their much-loved pumproom trio,
And sell postcards of unoccupied bikinis.
Will they be able also to decode
The stern prohibition on petting and horseplay,
Or to account for that funny, male strutting
At large through the changing-rooms? To rebuild
That miserable, suggestive, chlorinated ache
From girls trailing toes in the blue water?

THE GREEN PARTY

When the invite came I wasn't sure
Why I'd been asked. Who gave them my name?
And what did they stand for? There was,
I'd noticed in the streets, some stirring
Of the Easter lily, tucked furtively
Behind the lapel, like a pioneer pin
Before the social. Could that be it?

Everybody who was anyone was there
When I arrived, from Kavanagh expounding
The mystery of grass, to Donovan
Still harping on treachery. But who
Was the man in the hat, taking all in,
His sherry untouched? Eyes over shoulders,
Couldn't escape each other quick enough.

I too wanted out before the business
Started, but doors were closed. Two hours later,
Speeches finished, nothing was settled and I
None the wiser. The mixture as before:
Mushrooms, mushrooms, mushrooms. According to
    some
The heady whiff of the inch down by the river
As the clouds built up to the westward.

I'll tell you this much: when they take to the streets
They needn't think that I'll be falling in
Behind their primitive, vegetable cause.

THE NTH CIRCLE

'In this next circle are those made paranoid
By lacking due preferment in their jobs.'

The tourist's eyes strayed across the river
To the woods where the great suicides sat
Attempting to repair loose flaps of skin,
Or melancholy lovers ghosted behind trees.

The guide is running out of patience,
Anxious to press on towards Purgatory
Before nightfall. But how can she, with Paolo
Standing there, fix her attention on
These almost-people of Bloomusalem,
All getting each other into corners,
Describing their bad luck: how, between
You and me, but for one snap of the fingers
They'd have won that game, or round, or frame?

Their error's obvious: settling down in life,
They'd come to confuse the appointments section
With the obituaries. And here they are.

THE MUST-BELOVED

That blast from the past seems to sound again
Once per generation, defined as the time
It takes your daughter's first teeth to wear out.
A glimpse, perhaps, from a train window
As it roars up speed out of the station; or
A look at a party where you hope you'll stay
Sober enough not to go breasting up to her.
One night, though, in a smoky tube, rocking
Deafeningly through the gloom, a tired woman
Lolled asleep. Her, twenty years on? A likelier
Candidate, considering your own grey hair,
The uneven stripe of sun-tan round your sternum.

So where does it leave you? It leaves you hoping
No Avice or Iseult of your daughter's age
Will stand a pace away, tying your tongue.

ANAMNESIS

Each January you learn anew
How little cold it needs to be
For the raindrops slanting past
The window-pane to turn to snow;
And whether by preference you'd remember
From year to year, or settle for
This dreamer's pattern of forgetting
There is no call to know.

In budding-time you rediscover
The willow-warbler's shapely song
And the scent of resurrection in
The dried-out dust revived by rain.
In such games of Blind Man's Buff
Whoever stood behind your back,
Clasping their hands around your eyes,
Will always stop. You'll see again.

THE ABSENT SIGNIFIER

I'd always thought that, when we stayed in Bruges,
We missed the canals for which it's celebrated,
Until this postcard, ten years later, came.
Now, realising the unprepossessing stream
I could see from our high window was them,
I think: 'I should have had a camera'.

But why are we incapable of seeing
An inamorata, fritillaries in April,
Hekla, Herculaneum or Troy,
Without the wish to snap them and say 'mine'
Through photographs we hide away in albums –
Out of focus, ill-angled or too bright?

Because it proves this: that on the other side
Of the observing, perpetuating box
Was someone; and, since the camera was mine,
I must, at some juncture, have been there.
So: even if it isn't for the likes
Of us to hear the music of the spheres,

Yet this dim smudge of Halley's on the sky,
Like the thumbprint of a child messing
With lenses, suggests that behind the sheer,
Navy firmament, someone's indicating
With similar, posterior possessiveness
That he exists and has a world to prove it.

'GOATS AND MONKEYS!'

Observe the spider, doggo on his thread,
A drying husk that the wind could blow aside.
But if you're up early, you will catch him
Starting his day, letting out line silently.
I take my cap off to him, a brother
And a colleague: the thinking raptor,
Lying in wait, hatching plans, then striking.
Unlike the heron or ostrich, he is good at it.

The mouse I speak well of and affect
A liking for: with Jerry against Tom.
Watching him dance on a loose ceiling-board,
You have to laugh: 'he's so tame, he'd nearly
Talk to you'. But when I leave the house,
I place carefully sited plates of poison,
Obliterating everything of him except
The objectionable whiff of death.

As for the wasp, I cannot really take
To a creature that stands up for itself
With such aggression. I like his style:
His livery, his witty music,
His delicate fuselage. But the pay-off
Can't be helped, the quiet thud of petrol
At his nest. We can't have these small beasts
That strike us without dying in the act.

THE SAGA OF MCGUINNESS'S DOG

A man lived by the Araglen river
Called John Tim Jack. He kept the greyhounds for
The village doctor on his farm. The doctor,
As a man of substance, had a fridge before
The days of fridges, where he kept the dog-meat:
Bones, knuckles and unconvincing-looking
Daubs of red. John Tim's children tried to seize

The moment when the fridge light winked off.
The doctor, trundling in from his visits
To the pub, would list in the doorway, asking
'Are you sure the fridge light's out? Is the cow
Still in the grove?' Cows they knew well of old;
But the grove was attributed to drink
As they stole away and left him to reflect.

In February, when evenings first lengthened out,
School ended at two to let the scholars
Watch the coursing. John Tim brought the dogs,
Mad eyes and coats shining, lolling tongues
Looking too long to fit back in their heads.
They never won; but once his *Maggie's Fury*
Nearly made it. The children stood and cheered

Through the early rounds as hare after hare
Was ripped until the cold moon was noticed,
Rousing concern for dogs' legs in the frost.
Fury's opponent in the final had
A name (maybe false) no-one had heard of,
Entered by a stranger calling himself
McGuinness, with coat collar turned up.

Another hare made in a doomed scuttle
For the grass curtain at the course's end.
Fury was off like lightning over the glint
Of frost-grass to take the first turn in style.
But *Tanyard Subject* came from nowhere, winning
The second. The hare was killed. *Fury* was kicked
Back in his trailer for the dark drive home.

1159, when John of Salisbury
Writes in his *Metalogicon* about
The followers of Cornificius
(A name derived from Virgil's discommender)
Who 'pay no heed to what philosophy
Teaches, and what it shows that we should seek
Or shun. Their sole ambition', in the words
Of John, 'is making money: by fair means
If possible, but otherwise by any
Means at all. There's nothing they deem sordid
Or inane except the straits of poverty.
Wisdom's only fruit for them is wealth'.

So much for John of Salisbury – a classic case
Of a moralising, moaning so-called thinker.
But now a more hopeful fable for our time:
The case of the loganberry. After great
Creating nature did its bit, along came
Logan to supply the obvious defect:
A red blackberry with an elongated nose.
Everyone's happy: he makes a killing,
And Kate Potosi gets her cut by selling
Them to people to make jam. My point is this:

If John of Salisbury'd taken out a leaf
From Cornificius's book and used his brains
To come up with something practical like that,
He might have saved the whole of western Europe
Centuries of fruitless disputation.

THE NUTHATCH

I couldn't fathom why, one leafless
Cloudcast morning he appeared to me,
Taking time off from his rind-research
To spread his chestnut throat and sing
Outside my window. His woodwind
Stammering exalted every work-day
For weeks after. Only once more
I saw him, quite by chance, among
The crowding leaves. He didn't lift
His head as he pored over his wood-text.
Ashamed of the binocular intrusion,
Like breath on eggs or love pressed too far,
I'm trying to pretend I never saw him.

BITTERN

Ultimately sex, no doubt: like a drunk's
Drooled elegy across the rounded lips
Of an empty bottle. Standing, kind of,
Chin in the air, thick head swaying in time
To the wind. Soliciting nobody
For nothing, a real non-combatant.
He's trying to pass like Syrinx for a reed,
A daft civilian in a daft disguise.
Out of touch with his leggy womenfolk,
Those symbols of longevity: the keen heron,
The stiletto-shod crane stilting archly
Round the puddles, the pink-gorged flamingo
Dropping off on one leg, bored with alluring.

He can't be serious! Does he really think
The fowler at the break of day
Will take him for a tender grass and go?

MORNING IN BEARA

Towns, small islands, *domus* and *rus*
Is the rule in this last wedge of state
Sketched over by cartographers.
Angled houses through glassless frames
Overlook the sound where the gannet
Cuts out and falls. The curate
Developed a stammer; the economy
He founded foundered. His photos even
Were blurred, of this corner
Where no one comes on purpose.

Men came once, unwrapping bales
Of something on the beach. They glazed
The windows and repaired the thatch,
Starting a honey-farm in nine rows
Of cannabis. But the Council
Broke the windows, and in the rafters
Hung Vapona for the bees.

Back in the *status quo*, the old woman
Takes up her ageless beat again.
A mile or so out,
You can listen to the shingle's scramble
As the escaping pebbles lose their footing.

THE ATLANTEANS

September in West Cork and Flynn is burning,
Stamping mud off his feet and wasting matches.
His blue curl of smoke winds up against
The purple hills of Beara, adding
The last touch of elegy its beauty lacked.
Southward you can see the gulls trawl the wake
Of Harrington's boat where the mackerel
Have crowded in through Dursey Sound.

Harrington's cousin (R. I. P.) was drowned
Last week in Cork, a hundred miles east
(American papers please copy), when
He fell between the boatside and the dock.
Four hundred miles further east, I am at
Speaker's Corner, half-hearing an Arab's
Cryptic challenge to the old-time socialist
Who'd asked for questions from the Hyde Park idlers.

'When you gain power, will you give Ireland back
To Morocco?', his query reinforced
By the music writhing out of his transistor.
Such territorial problems are nothing
To do with me; I'm just scanning *The Tribune*
For team news, prior to watching
The All-Ireland final in the Odeon,
Praying to God they won't let us down again.

But whose responsibility is it,
This Celt/Atlantic business? When Poseidon's
Allotted share exploded in the prehistoric,
Unrecorded cataclysm, leaving
A keel-entrapping undertow of mud,
How did they part, to leave Morocco perched
On Africa's shoulder, while feckless Ireland
Drifted towards trouble in the northern gales?

Still, I've heard it said, if you close your eyes
And listen hard in Marrakech or Fez
You will hear wafted out of the bazaars
The Lament for Staker Wallace. North, and
The sulphurous curl of smoke gave its name
To Reykjavik, where the cathedral roof
Is made (I ask you!) of green galvanise,
As used for henhouses or for fencing gaps.

From Agadir, to Castletownberehaven,
To Reykjanes, nothing's been finished right
From top to bottom of this wretched seaboard.
When civilisation crept north and eastward
To set up buildings, working its way
From capital to capital, it lost heart
Before it got this far. Flynn with his matches
And the gravediggers, mourning caps in hand,

Are destroying the evidence. But if
'Art raises its head where creeds relax',
What did art do here while God rested
His weary bones? Snakes banned by Patrick
Are charmed from baskets in North Africa
And frozen next to fishes in the margins
Of our dead manuscripts. Icelanders
Sit over fires and wait for renewal of

The fateful query 'Is Gunnar at home?',
Boding quietus, whether from land or sea.
After defeat in the final, I loll
Towards sleep on the M40, drummed by that
Curious social peace you get at night
On buses among strangers, attempting
To put those images together,
As if the creator never had let up.

SOUVENIRS

'*Tá an lá go breá*!' 'You have the Irish well.
An bhfuil souvenirs uait? Here I have
Souvenirs my own hands made, from shells
Found westward on the Aran beaches,
Not on this island only, but as well
On Inishmeán and Inishmore'.

He led me past his father who was sitting
In the sun, looking with the satisfaction
Of a tourist over the sea. Pieces
Of crooked copper wire (as it were Celtic
Torques, shrunken like toy dogs from the miracles
Displayed in the National Museum)

Were spread on his wiped kitchen oilcloth.
'Would souvenirs be pleasing to your wife
Or to your children? Children often like
Souvenirs'. All I had in my pocket
Smaller than fivers were three golden
English pounds, and I offered them.

'English money is all right too. We change
It for Irish in the Galway banks,
Or at the mobile bank that stops longside
The music pub in Doolin'. Now they're on a shelf
Here in my study, and all I can recall
Is wondering if his English came from Synge.

Line 1: 'It's a fine day!'
Line 2: Would you like some souvenirs?

CROKE PARK OR BALLYLEE, 1989

We propped a bed against the grainloft door
To keep the cats out so the second brood
Of swallows could escape to the power-lines;
But as the end of holiday approached,
We watched more anxiously each day that passed
The swaying, squawking line of them
On the rafters over the cheery birdlime.

We changed the return ferry booking
To extend our guard; and then, one evening
We got back from Galleycove with the sea
Still washing in our ears to find them gone.
Mystery, relief and minor heartache.
They'd left one last decision to be made:
How to spend these extra, God-given days

With the best that Ireland had to offer.
Should we go up to the All-Ireland final,
Or repeat another tried pilgrimage:
The Tarbert ferry, pause at Craggaunowen
To see the Brendan, on past Dysert O'Dea,
And through the Burren to Yeats's Tower
To watch the moorhens from the lancet windows?

It was a question, as we packed the car,
Of which would season better through the nights
Of coming winter: 'they nobbled Tompkins';
'Allen was past it'; or 'you can still see
The winding stair and breathe the mice and damp
Above the starling's nest where "Meditations
In Time of Civil War" was written'.

Look for guidance to the swallows, still
Protesting against ravishment, now from
Their wire-platforms high above the scabious,
Or weaving their telling tapestries
Of air, sticking still to the same story,
Unchanged since last year or last age, after
Their sally from the loft. Here in the uplands

They're safe from the stonechat's mockery
And still the theme of Yeatsian meditation
As they soar away from the old woman's house,
A ruin by a clogged straw tumulus.
In the event we were driving down the bleak
Central plain, straining to hear the commentary
From Dublin above the engine noise.

On a whim we switched it off and turned for Gort,
And walked in Coole woods, trying to distinguish seven.
We took slips of three rhododendrons and watched
The lake through the mulberry, debating
Uncertainly which was the house and which
The servants' quarters. When we turned on again,
It was just too late to hear the final score.

WULF AND EADWACER

You'd think they were doing us a favour
With their custody. One word though
And we're both finished. We're done for.

So here I am in polite conversation
While you patrol that dark island,
Set in its ways: mist and bog all round,
And the people killers to a man.
Just raise your head, and they have you.
We're done for all right.

It seems only yesterday they were all
Smiles: 'it must be delightful there
This time of year'. I'd gladly
Burn for you, my far-off Wulf,
If that would do them.

It was raining, I remember; when you
First took my hand, my stomach clenched
With fear and joy. The backlash
Was inevitable. Ah Wulf, Wulf, my Wulf!
Now my stomach dies with longing
And shrivels at the memory of those days.

No doubt your ear's stuck to the keyhole,
Civil jailor! So now you know: a wolf
Holds in the wilds what should be
The token of our union. It's easy enough,
God knows, to sunder pieces that never
Clung together, like the notes
Of our discordant poor duet.

CASEMENT ON BANNA

In this dawn waking, he is Oisin
Stretching down for the boulder
That will break his girth and plunge
Him into age; he's Columcille
Waiting for foreign soil to leak
From his sandals and bring him death
In Ireland. He can't be roused
By any fear of danger once he's started
His own laying-out on this white sand.

Watching the usual landmarks in the sky,
He can no longer place them. Is that
Pegasus? Where's Orion? Surer of
The wash and whisper from the Maharees,
He spots the oyster-catcher going off
To raise the alarm: an insane Orpheus
Craving a past he'd never had. His quest
Beached here that started in mutilation
And manacled rubber-harvesters.

Suddenly it has thrown him on the ground,
A man sick with his past, middled-aged,
Mad, more or less, who waits to be lifted
High, kicking in mid-air, gurgling
For breath, swaying, while Banna's lonely sand
Drips for the last time from his shoe. So:
Was this the idea? The cure for every woe,
Injustice, brutishness? In this ecstasy
Larks rising everywhere, as he'd forgotten.

P.T.A.

'Parent Teacher Association'.
Ganging up on the innocent,
Sounds like to me. When Lear turns nasty –
'Take heed, sirrah! The whip!' –
I recognize the voice of those
Weird fathers who urged the teacher
'Give them the stick and plenty of it.'

Easy to talk, of course. Maybe
That was the best education
For their lives: suitcases
Upturned on customs desks;
Cross-examination by people,
Themselves fearful, who hate
Without understanding.

PARLIAMENT OF FOWLS

Personally, I don't feel all that *tristis*
Post coitum; if anything it enhances
That sense of genial complacency
Which is my hallmark. Often (I'm talking now
Of the time since I gave up smoking),
Middle of the night though it be, I take off
For a walk to listen to the birds:
Thrushes, chaffinches, nuthatches – the works.
You probably didn't know about them
Singing through the night. You can stand
And watch them, clear as day, and happy
As the day is long: the tree-creeper,
Poking and sipping away; the dipper
With his shoulder eye-twitch; woodpeckers
Drumming (pied) or yaffling (green:
Possibly the other way around: it's
The middle of the night, remember);
The kingfisher patrolling the dark
Like a gyroscoping emergency light.

I know what you're thinking: you're thinking
'He's making it all up, like the brother's
Stories of your men the seals, conversing
And smoking upstairs in the trams.'
All I can say is: 'Try me. Come to my room
And give me half a chance. See what I propose
And what it leads to. After all, what else
Can you do with the empty, early hours
Past midnight, alone and weeping like the plowman?'

HOLY ISLAND

Bells ringing over the water
Make sweeter music and carry
More strongly to greater distance

At Mass time, when at home I'd escape
With rose clippings to the Council dump,
I walked by the shore where turnstones
Rolled along the sand like a spilt rosary
And merry clouds of knot veered through the sea's
Splash of light, like guilt-arousing girls
On holiday with skirts tucked up,
Pushing, shrieking, linked at the elbow.

Across the shell-debris beach the island
Where the saint bestowed his soul.
Twice a day it edges towards the land
And backs away again, like a child learning fear,
Unsure of its welcome. Pilgrim cormorants,
Like stigmata-seekers, lift out their wings
Showing their blue-black, unsandalled feet.

No nightingale, no thrush in the blue evening
Will serenade this tattered cross
Tolling its barren silence over the sound.

THE POTTER'S FIELD

With better luck he might have been a saint
Or, failing that, lived richly on the interest,
Since thirty silver pieces is a lot.
Yet he flung his fortune back on principle
And, weeping, ran away and hanged himself.
Hearing that tale the first time, any child
Might well, until instructed, cry at his fate.

So what made him the byword for a traitor,
Forever gnawed by thin-lipped Dante's Satan?
Observe the lettering above the gate:
'Iscariot's cemetery for foreign nationals'.
Bequests like his win no one love; their need's
Resented, like a prostitute's caress
Consigned by its beneficiary to Hell.

Somewhere near Rockall in the western ocean,
There is a crag that spits the Atlantic's spray
Back in its face. There, once a century,
Judas sits for the night, his lips refleshing
In the wind, craving the beads of water
He sees hang in every purple clapper
Down endless avenues of seaboard fuchsia.

My tears-of-god bloom as red here beside
The Queen Elizabeth and Iceberg roses
As on their native drywall back in Kerry.
The soil's hospitable; the air is delicate.
So I think that now I'm well enough heeled in
To rate a plot inside the graveyard wall,
Escaping Giudecca. Accursèd be his name!

III MALADIES

THE WEAKNESS

It was the frosty early hours when finally
The cow's despairing groans rolled him from bed
And into his boots, hardly awake yet.
He called 'Dan! come on, Dan!
She's calving', and stumbled without his coat
Down the icy path to the haggard.

Castor and Pollux were fixed in line
Over his head but he didn't see them,
This night any more than another.
He crossed to the stall, past the corner
Of the fairy-fort he'd levelled last May.
But this that stopped him, like the mind's step

Backward: what was that, more insistent
Than the calf's birth-pangs? 'Hold on, Dan.
I think I'm having a weakness.
I never had a weakness, Dan, before.'
And down he slid, groping for the lapels
Of the shocked boy's twenty-year old jacket.

CON CORNIE

in memoriam

A farmer's fingers on a flageolet,
Bunched, too crowded, but weaving
A seamless tapestry of sound. A glide
Through a drift of touch, a slur conceded
By a wise, sideways moving of the head.

What complaint was stitched on to the air –
What child bereaved or wife sorrowing –
Was not his part now, intent on making
A fling of notes you could broadcast anywhere.

THE HUMOURS OF SHRONE

The peregrine's anxious *kai* hangs
In the air-bowl of the mountains
Over the limestone lake, water so black
That even in heatwave summer it dims
The sun. There, eighty years ago

On Christmas Eve our young neighbour pulled
His horse's jawing head
Into the blizzard for the eight miles
Of nodding, doddering at the reins
With his swirling load of quicklime.

The red candle in the window was burnt through,
Its warm hole in the frost veil closed
Before his sister heard in the haggard
The frenzied horse clashing his traces
Down the stone yard and the jagged

Shafts leaping behind, trying to keep up.
They found the boy next morning in our quarry
In the snow, with blind holes lime-burned in his face.
So the sister said: ninety, doting and inclined
To roam the quarry-field to search again.

ROUND THE CAMPFIRE

The grassy bridge, cut off now
By the new road's sweep, is
My daughter's memorial:
The undergrowth still fused
To half-burnt tin and
Non-biodegradable plastic.

At Appleby she darted laughing
From the van, dodging hooves
Better than anyone. She sang
'Dingle Bay' all down the M1
On our way to run the gauntlet
Of the customs.

Why it was going to Puck Fair
She died, I couldn't say.
She knew the road well; she ran
No quicker from the shelter
Of the van; the car that hit
Her went no faster.

We put her on the sheets,
And gathered in the caravan
Our every last possession off
The hedges. The dogs
And horses roared blue murder
As the fire took the household

Down to bone-handled knives
Her mother's crimson scarf,
Pillows the children fought with,
And the carved chairs we'd found
On the street in Cheltenham
And never traced an owner for.

Waiting in the Social Security
For 50p's, I kept thinking
Of a night when she woke up
Screaming 'The fire! The fire!
Mind my bed! Take my bed out
To the cool of the roadside!'

THE FOOL IN THE GRAVEYARD

*When we die, we help each other out
Better than usual.*

This was his big day, and he was glad
His Dad was dead, because everyone,
However important or usually
Unfriendly, came up to him and
Solemnly shook his new leather glove
And said 'I'm sorry for your trouble'.
No trouble at all. All these people
Who normally made fun of him
And said, 'What's your name, Dan?'
And laughed when he said 'Dan' (wasn't
That right and polite?), were nice as pie
Today. He'd missed him going to bed
But they'd given him a pound and
An apple and told him a joke.

That made him laugh a bit.
Coming down the aisle, he'd been
At the front with the coffin on
His shoulder, and everyone
Without exception looked straight
At him, some of them nodding gravely
Or mouthing 'How's Dan', and even
Crying, some of them. He'd tried
To smile and nod back, anxious
To encourage kindness. Maybe
They'd always be nice now, remembering
How he'd carried the coffin. Outside
It was very cold, but he had on
The Crombie coat his Dad had bought.

The earth was always yellower
Here than anywhere else, heaped
Next to the grave with its very
Straight sides. How did they dig
The sides so straight? The priest
Led the prayers, and he knew most
Of the answers. Things were looking up.
Today he was like the main actor
In the village play, or the footballer
Who took the frees, or the priest
On the altar. Every eye
Fixed on him! It was like being loved,
And he'd always wondered what that was like.
It wasn't embarrassing at all.

KATE'S ROSES

For her they grew as freely as her stories,
Their heavy scent as palpable as words,
So we all took slips to graft them to
Our less expressive ditches. And, though we were
Ignorant of the variety, sometimes
They'd take root. Hardly a note in her head,
Yet she was a great singer of tales.

She cried at the end of *Tess of the d'Urbervilles*
And prayed for the fictional recovery
Of Mrs Kennedy of Castlerosse.
While her Mullard crackled out the BBC
As the royal couple cantered down The Mall,
She sighed 'It's nice for the old king to have
One of them done for.' But who took up the narrative

When she died? Who then pruned story and rose alike?
She'd delight to compose a long lament
Which would embrace the whole legendary
Of mourners: the egg-man with his fierce,
Hooked weighing-scales and gallon wodged with notes,
Protected by his evil Kerry Blue;
That ghost who breathed cold, visible clouds

Behind her husband in the horse and trap
Crossing the storied Blackwater; the hares
That boxed defiance as a sign. Who else?
Her house now is the soul of discretion
When we shoulder aside the door and its zinc
Strip screeches on the flagstone. No radio;
No wind-up HMV; not even the great

Dominant dresser in the cool, lace-hallowed Room.
We've looked all day for the roses, hoping
To identify the species from a book.
But even if we did make them out, maybe
We'd find by now they have chronic maladies
And have to make up our own names for them:
'Dearth', 'Tongue-tied', 'Poverty', or 'Childlessness'.

COWBOYS

Showing up soon in a battered van parked
In your area: shears-sharpeners and
Tree-trimmers, begging to do you favours.
No V.A.T., no insurance-numbers;
In the interests of your economy
Nothing passes through the books. For some reason
(I leave you to fill in the connexion)
They hopelessly recall a village case,
The man who won the tractor-backing at
The yearly carnival and showered children
With small change and hay-float rides, anxious
That the ravelling ropes shouldn't chafe their legs.
One Friday night he played the fruit-machine,
Hoping to win in the end so much that
The days of all his days should reach perfection,
Until the last DHSS half-crown
Winked derision at him, and the barman called
Closing-time. The doors chinked to behind him
On meaningless laughter, and he staggered off
To (quite an achievement, this) drown himself
In eighteen inches of river during a drought.

DOWN SYNDROME

i. m. Joseph Leary

Right from the cradle it had been observed
You didn't grasp fingers hard enough;
Your smiles came all too readily,
Dispensed without prescription.
But sleep well, Joseph, and don't weep
For your pale eyes or your weakness
For the truth.

Take consolation that it won't be you
That has to declare strategy
Or give the order to burn sprawling
Ranks of soldiers. You're not even
In the running, poor old Joseph,
In the competition to achieve
Such grand affliction.

Keep to your first love: inspire again
Someone to give you the front seat
And drive west with the radio blaring;
Left at the grotto through the rushy wastes
Where the weak heads of cotton
Barely survive the scattering breeze
Off Shrone Lake.

I have a plan: on Easter Saturday
We'll pull up by the verge where the view
Is longest across to the mountains
And listen out for the first willow-wrens.
We'll see the daffodils that come
Before the swallow dares and take –
Take what

That we would wish untaken?
Words, maybe, to straighten out
Your energetic tongue and our
Crookeder tongues, so between us
We can name the things worth naming
And cure our more aspiring
Elocutionary malady.

NOT I : SHE!

Not that she could recall, but someone must
Have left a door open. The wind that blew in,
Disordering her hair, had a damp edge
Of clay to it that chilled her wits away.
There was someone too they wheeled from room to
   room,
Who fell downstairs last night and broke their wrist:
A tourist, maybe, who'd put her passport down
And couldn't find it now in this dark land;
Perhaps a husband who'd had one too much
And couldn't hold his key.

She was coiffured,
Chiropodised. They must be admirers,
These men in longs coats, gathering like bees
Around a honey-pot while she still wound
And unwound her thread. Those places she's called home
Had crystal walls: all now long drives away,
As round her arm the nurses wrapped a plaster
Winding-sheet, which must have some significance.

MADONNAS

Like a girl at a summer language-school
Making her arms an unnatural platform
For ring-bound folders, the best carry
Their child inexpertly, looking away,
Being ignorant that the garish goldfinch
In his fist denotes his fate on Calvary
Or city-street or battlefield. Some hold on
With desperate, fated protectiveness,
Refusing to respect his father's business.

One, of brown ivory, lowers her eyes
To her empty lap, to the rupture where
One leg of mannered draping and small,
Chiselled toes flow from her right side.
Her own arm is missing on the left,
Perhaps because she clung more tightly to
The innocent than his own human limbs.
But you wouldn't know, so far away
Her eyes which don't yet grasp her tragedy.

DEATH

You took it in because you thought you heard
A rattle under the bonnet: nothing more.
A minor service – not the 12,000 one.
Collecting it at five, you can't believe
The engine's done, the valves not reparable.
'We could try a decoke – see if we can raise
The compression. But it's expensive,
And I'm not promising anything, mind.'

Worth a try; but of course you know the truth.
A few thousand more, at best, and you'll be rolling it
Down to the back wall of the scrapyard.
You'll try not to look back, and curse yourself
For a childish and sentimental fool.

KINDERTOTENLIEDER

Because we cannot see into the future,
It follows that what we anticipate
Can't happen. And so I've set myself
Imagining the worst that can be feared:
The child beneath her bike, the wheel still spinning;
Another deathbed, not in a curtain-cooled
Summer afternoon with farm-voices outside,
But foetid in a northern city
In December. I've watched my children's classmates
Wearing ties, lined up by hissing teachers.

But I find the point is passing where I can
Switch from this Hyde life and smiling watch them pore
Over the *Beano*. The mind too is a country
Like Somalia. The fly that a slow hand
Pushes from a lip again, again,
Will hold its ground and crawl towards an eyelid
That fails at last to keep up appearances
By opening to resume its death's stare.

ESPRIT DE L'ESCALIER

I thought he was the gardener as he bent
Over the roses. Fingering for leaf-scars,
He told me of a loud continuous hum
Inside his head, which a knowing man
Had told him (in total confidence)
Came from the tension generated
By the conflict of two great powers.
What powers, the wise man hadn't said.

Stuck for an answer, I only thought of
Brain tumours and how these unbudded roses
Would fade upon his grave. But should have said
How wonderful it was what wise men knew
Denied the rest of us, and how the roots
Of roses live on through a hundred half-years.

VANELLUS, VANELLUS

When I'd forgotten them, you told me how
I saw them in the morning going to school,
Tattering down the sallow sky of winter.
Now I know them well: I see them every mile
By flocks and companies in roadside fields
As I drive onwards through these snowcast days
To sit at your bed evoking them for you.

MUNSTER FINAL

in memory of Tom Creedon, died 28 August 1983

The jarveys to the west side of the town
Are robbers to a man, and if you tried
To drive through The Gap, they'd nearly strike you
With their whips. So we parked facing for home
And joined the long troop down the meadowsweet
And woodbine-scented road into the town.
By blue Killarney's lakes and glens to see
The white posts on the green! To be deafened
By the muzzy megaphone of Jimmy Shand
And the testy bray to keep the gangways clear.

As for Tom Creedon, I can see him still,
His back arching casually to field and clear.
'Glory Macroom! Good boy, Tom Creedon!'
We'd be back next year to try our luck in Cork.

We will be back next year, roaring ourselves
Hoarse, praying for better luck. After first Mass
We'll get there early; that's our only hope.
Keep clear of the carparks so we're not hemmed in,
And we'll be home, God willing, for the cows.

LASTWORDA BETST

So many ways (formal, political,
Witty) of writing poems not on the theme
Of dead parents, it's surprising how many
Have fallen into the trap. Odd too
To find on waking this anniversary
Morning my eyelids – tearless and well-slept –
Were hot to the touch. A *midrash*, maybe,
Whose prophecy is found twenty-four years
Back, at the March-wind final whistle
Of a football-match when, dull and emptied
Like a flask, I watched the crush-barriers
Reappear among celebrating Cork fans.
Their voice rose up, leaving the cold body
With our small company. I've never heard
My christian name without a start again
Since he stopped and shouted it, his last word.

A NOTED JUDGE OF HORSES

The ache in his right arm worsening
Morning by morning asks for caution.
He knows its boding, cannot be wrong
About this. Yet he is more concerned
For the planks in the float that need
Woodworm treatment before drawing in
The hay, and whether the coarse meadow
Must be limed before it will crop again.

Still in the pallid dawn he dresses
In the clothes she laid out last night,
Washes in cold water and sets off,
Standing in the trailer with his eyes set
On the Shrove Fair. As long as his arm
Can lift a stick to lay in judgement
Down the shuddering line of a horse's back,
He'll take his chance, ignoring his dream
That before September's fair he'll be mumbling
From a hospital bed, pleading with nurses
To loose the pony tied by the western gate.